# T
# Bestest EVER
# Bear X

First published 2010
by Walker Books Ltd
87 Vauxhall Walk
London SE11 5HJ

2 4 6 8 10 9 7 5 3 1

Text © year of publication individual authors
as noted in the acknowledgements

Illustrations © 2010 Colin West

The right of Colin West to be identified as illustrator of this Work
has been asserted by him in accordance with the Copyright,
Designs and Patents Act 1988

This book has been typeset in Maiandra GD Roman

Printed and bound in Great Britain
by Clays Ltd, St Ives plc

Paper kindly supplied free of charge
by Paper Management Services

All rights reserved.

British Library Cataloguing in Publication Data:
a catalogue record for this book is available
from the British Library

ISBN 978-1-4063-2973-5

www.walker.co.uk

# The Bestest Bear ^Ever

## Bear

Chosen and illustrated
by Colin West

WALKER BOOKS
AND SUBSIDIARIES

LONDON · BOSTON · SYDNEY · AUCKLAND

# Foreword

*The Bestest Ever Bear* has got to be the bestest ever book of bear poems. It is illuminated ever more by the wonderful illustrations of Colin West, which will have great appeal for both children and adults – especially those who love their teddy bears!

Best of all, profits from the sale of this book will help to enhance the lives of some very special children at The Children's Trust who receive care, education and therapy – including children with acquired brain injuries.

I hope that you will get as much fun out of reading these poems as I did. This book is a delightful read. Enjoy!

**Phil Tufnell**
Vice President
The Children's Trust

# Contents

# The Children's Trust

A very special bear became the figurehead for a campaign almost a generation ago that has changed the lives of thousands of children. The bear's name is *Taddy* and he has helped to draw the public's attention to the needs of some of the UK's most disabled youngsters. Thanks to Taddy's efforts and the hard work of a group of like-minded people, The Children's Trust was established to provide nursing care, education and therapy for severely disabled children.

The Children's Trust started the UK's first rehabilitation service to help children who have suffered a brain injury

following a very serious accident or illness. Our special school, St Margaret's, has developed and published a new way of teaching children with the most severe disabilities and 'Profound Education' now helps hundreds of young people here and abroad.

Photograph © Keith Walter

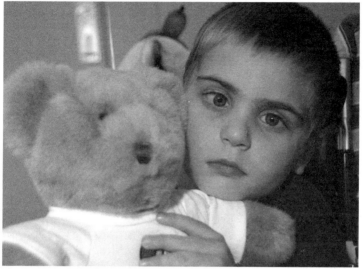

*Photograph © Andy Newbold Photography*

Sales of *The Bestest Ever Bear* will help The Children's Trust to reach out to more children. There are thousands who could benefit from our knowledge and expertise but reaching them depends on raising money. Most of all, this book provides us with the opportunity to enjoy some wonderful poems, something all children get pleasure from – especially snuggled down with their "bestest ever" bear.

My thanks go to Walker Books for their commitment and hard work, to all the poets included and to Colin West for all his enthusiasm and support for this book.

**Liz Haigh-Reeve**
Director of Fundraising & Communications
The Children's Trust

# Introduction

*Little Miss Muffet sat on a tuffet,*
*Eating a fabulous lunch.*
*It wasn't a spider who sat down beside her,*
*But thirty big bears in a bunch!*

There are thirty big (and not-so-big)
bears in this book to help celebrate
thirty years of Walker Books.

So read aloud in your bestest
bear voice and smile!

## Fuzzy Wuzzy

Fuzzy Wuzzy was a bear,
A bear was Fuzzy Wuzzy.
When Fuzzy Wuzzy lost his hair,
He wasn't fuzzy, was he?

**Anon**

# Furry Bear

If I were a bear,
  And a big bear too,
I shouldn't much care
  If it froze or snew;
I shouldn't much mind
  If it snowed or friz –
I'd be all fur-lined
  With a coat like his!

**A.A. Milne**

# Honey Bear

There was a big bear
Who lived in a cave;
His greatest love
Was honey.
He had twopence a week
Which he never could save,
So he never had
Any money.
I bought him a money box
Red and round,
In which to put
His money.
He saved and saved
Till he got a pound,
Then spent it all
On honey.

**Elizabeth Lang**

# Limerick

There was an Old Person of Ware,

Who rode on the back of a bear;

When they ask'd, "Does it trot?" –

He said, "Certainly not!

He's a Moppsikon Floppsikon bear!"

**Edward Lear**

# The Bestest Bear Song

Oh,
this is the
bear,
the very best
bear,
the best *bestest* best
bear
of all.
It's lost one leg
and it's lost one eye
and it's spotty
and it's grotty
and it's small.
But
this is the
bear,
the very best
bear,
the best *bestest* best
bear
of all.
Yes, Sir!

It's wobbly and worn
and its left ear is torn
but it's been with me
since the day I was born
and I love,
oh, I love
its soft fur.
For
this is the
bear,
the very best
bear,
the best *bestest* best
bear
of all!
Yes, Sir!

**Wes Magee**

# Sir Grizzly

My name
Is Bear;

Sir Grizzly
to you.
Endear-
Endear-
Ingly
Cuddly,
But beware.
I instil
Fear
And can kill
With a hug.

Come closer,
My good man.
Have we been introduced?

I am dying
To shake your hand.

**John Agard**

# Hair-Bear

As I sat in his chair
    and his razor went whirr
and his scissors jabbered
    around my ears,
I saw in the mirror
    how snippings of my hair
fell to the floor
    in a tufty shower,
a hirsute downpour,
    and landing there
joined with the hair
    and wisps of beard
that had been cut earlier
    to make an ever-swirlier
flood of fur,
    all textures and colours,
that, somewhat to my terror,
    rose higher and higher,
till at last I heard
    the barber murmur,
"Will that be all, Sir?"

and the hair on the floor
appeared to gather
        itself together
with a mighty shudder,
        before – I swear –
leaping into the air
        in the shape of a bear
that marched to the door
        and, with a roar,
slouched off ...
        who knows where?

**Christopher Reid**

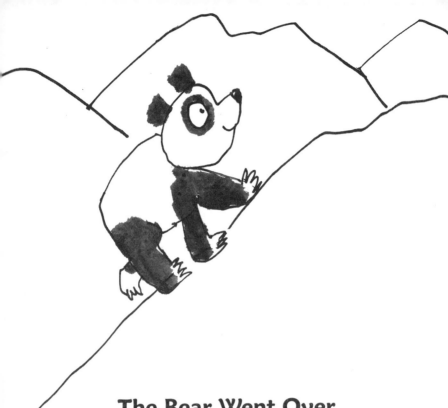

## The Bear Went Over the Mountain

The bear went over the mountain,

The bear went over the mountain,

The bear went over the mountain,

To see what he could see ...

The other side of the mountain,

The other side of the mountain,

The other side of the mountain,

That's all that he could see ...

**Anon**

## Polar Bear

Polar bear, polar bear,
How do you keep so clean?
You always seem to stay so white
No matter where you've been.

My mummy scrubs me every night
To wash the dirt away.
Somehow it all comes back again
When I go out and play.

Polar bear, polar bear,
Do you ever bath?
I seem to get so dirty
Just walking up the path.

I wish I was a polar bear,
So then every night
If someone tried to bath me,
I'd growl at them and bite!

**Spike Milligan**

# Runny Honey

Grab some pollen Mister Bumblebee.
Build a honeycomb and drop it on me.
I want that
Runny Honey.
Runny Honey
Makes my tummy feel fine and funny.

Bumblebee Bumblebee don't be late;
I'm not the kind of bear that likes to wait.
Bring me that
Runny Honey.
Runny Honey
Makes my tummy feel fine and funny.

Back in the cave my mama used to say
"You need that honey seven times a day".
I asked her if she meant the solid kind –
She said: "Bear, are you out of your mind?"
You need
Runny Honey,
Runny Honey.
Go slurp, slurp, slurp,
Then give a sweet burp
And eat that honey
While it's runny, Sonny.
That'll make your tummy feel fine, fine, fine
And funny!"

**Adrian Mitchell**

# The Small Brown Bear

The small brown bear

fishes

with stony paws

eating ice salmon

all waterfall slippery

till his teeth ache.

**Michael Baldwin**

# The Brown Bear

In the dark wood,
In a clearing,
Sleeps a brown bear,
Dreaming, dreaming.

His skin is furless,
His paws are clawless,
He walks into the city,
Lawless, lawless.

The moon is hidden,
The clouds are weeping,
A princess slumbers,
Sleeping, sleeping.

The thief creeps through
The royal bedroom
And steals her ruby,
A priceless heirloom.

The ruby glows
With fire and lightning,
A spell is cast,
So frightening, frightening.

The thief grows fur,
His body thickens,
His hands grow claws
He sickens, sickens.

Beneath the black sky
Thunder rumbles,
Into the dark wood
He stumbles, stumbles.

For in the ruby,
Gleaming, gleaming,
A wizard's mind
Is scheming, scheming.

Now, in the dark wood,
In a clearing,
Sleeps a brown bear,
Dreaming, dreaming.

**Roger Stevens**

# A Cold Snack

A polar bear, fed up with fish,
Decided to eat flowers
And searched across the snowy wastes
For hours and hours and hours.

Until at last he found a snowdrop
Growing through the ice.
A pretty flower but, thought the bear,
Just right for lunch, just nice.

He curled his paw to snatch it up,
Then stopped … was that a squeak?
And nosing close he saw the snowdrop
Nod and start to speak:

"Oh, Mr Bear, I know I'm small
And you are like a hill,
But if you take one bite of me
I'm sure to make you ill.

"Your fur will turn all greeny-grey,
Loud clangs will fill your head
And when you try to walk your feet
Will feel like lumps of lead.

"You won't know north from east or west,
You won't know left from right
And awful dreams of kangaroos
Will wake you up at night."

The bear stepped back and rubbed a paw
Across his worried face,
Then grunted, turned and loped away
To find his fishing place;

While all around the blizzard wailed
And cruel winds loudly blew,
So no one in the whole, white world
Could hear the snowdrop's: "Phew!"

**Richard Edwards**

# Grizzly Bear

If you ever, ever, ever meet a grizzly bear,
You must never, never, never ask him *where*
He is going.
Or *what* he is doing;
For if you ever, ever dare
To stop a grizzly bear,
You will never meet *another* grizzly bear.

**Mary Austin**

# Paws

My gloves are woollen paws
My mother knitted for me
While we were watching
TV after tea.

They keep me as warm
In the winter cold
As the fur of the big white bears
Who live in the ice and snow.

**Stanley Cook**

# Little Barbara

Little Barbara went to Scarborough,
Just to buy a candelabra.
At the harbour a bear ate Barbara.
Don't you find that most macabre?

**Colin West**

# A Cheerful Old Bear

A cheerful old bear at the Zoo

Could always find something to do.

When it bored him, you know,

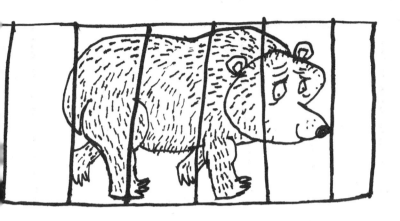

To walk to and fro,

He reversed it, and walked fro and to.

**Anon**

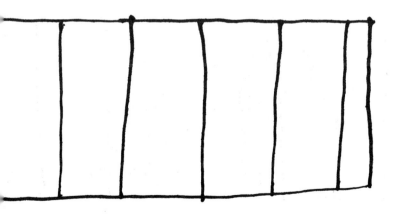

# Roberta Hyde

The trouble with Roberta Hyde
Was she was never satisfied.
She'd criticise the whole day long,
Everything was always *WRONG*.
"I don't like this. I don't like that.
I don't want a dog – I want a cat.
This pudding's cold – I want it hot.
I want the things I haven't got!"
Her suff'ring parents meekly tried
To keep their offspring satisfied,
A task that was gargantuan –
It just went on and on and on.

One day into the countryside
The family went for a ride.
They'd packed the car with things to eat –
Buttered scones and luncheon meat –
And when a pretty spot they found
They spread the picnic on the ground.
Roberta (who was always rude)
Said, "Shan't eat *that* – it's horrid food."
Her parents with a weary sigh
Didn't ask the reason why,
But said instead, "Don't wander, dear,
The woods are wild, so stay right here."

Roberta, though, was never good
And wandered off into the wood.

Alas, by chance, she passed the lair
Of a large and hungry bear.
The beast (he didn't mean to hurt her)
Stuck out a paw and grabbed Roberta.
His mouth he opened very wide
And popped the little girl inside.
Later on, he told his chums,
"The infant really wasn't yums –
Hardly sweet, a trifle tough
And there wasn't quite enough."

**Mark Burgess**

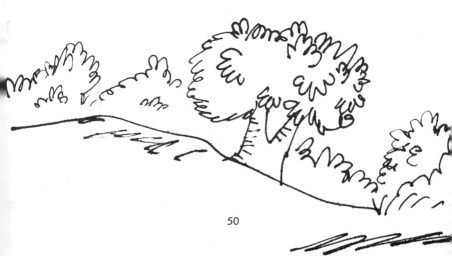

# 5 Ways to Stop Grizzly Bears from Spoiling Your Picnic

1. Shoe them away.

2. Lend them your teddy bears to play with.

3. Have food that grizzly bears don't like
   (e.g. fish heads ... donkey drops ...
   rat toenails ... frog eyes ... pig whiskers ...
   baboon bellybuttons ... bat milk ...).
   Definitely NOT honey!

4. Have the picnic in a country where
   there aren't any grizzly bears:
   South America for instance.
   (But watch out for tarantulas, crocodiles,
   boa constrictors, giant hamsters and
   child-eating goldfish!)

5. Learn a few grizzly bear phrases, like "Grrr"[1]
   and "Grr, Grr"[2] and "GRRRRRRRR"[3].

[1] "Good Afternoon."
[2] "I'm sorry, this is a private picnic."
[3] "Scram, or I shall call the armed militia."

**Roger McGough**

# Rare Bear

My Night Ted got this little hole,
It just appeared one day –
I said, "If we ignore it, Ted
It's bound to go away."
Imagine then my horror when
I next dragged him about,
I found that almost all of him
That was inside was out.
I called up M.U.M. for help,
"EMERGENCY? IT'S TED!
I think you should come quickly
With your needle and your thread."
Well, Mum got busy stitching;
A hundred's what it took
Or that is what she thought it was,
I couldn't bear to look.
And when at last she said, "That's done."
I didn't dare remark.
He hardly seemed like Ted at all,
But more like Noah's Ark.
She'd stitched him up and patched and darned
And saved him from the dump,

But on the way he'd lost a neck
And gained a camel's hump.
His nose was far less nose than snout,
His tum was slipping south.
There was a kind of penguin look
About his eyes and mouth.

I choked, I must apologise
But Mum said, "There's no need,
I think we've prob'ly seen to where
Ignoring holes can lead."
And Ted just blinked as if to say
"It wasn't such a crime;
I wouldn't be this rare new bear
If I'd been stitched in time."

**Hiawyn Oram**

# On a Trip Through Yellowstone

On a trip through Yellowstone,
Desmond held his ice-cream cone
Out for grizzly bears to savour.
Desmond's now their favourite flavour.

**X.J. Kennedy**

# A Bear is Not Disposed

A bear is not disposed

to dressing up in clothes,

not even underwear –

a bear likes being bare.

**Jack Prelutsky**

# I'm Much Better Than You

My dad's bigger than your dad,
Got more money too.
My house is posher than your house –
I'm much better than you.

My mum's prettier than your mum,
Our car is faster too.
We have a house in the country –
I'm much better than you.

My toys cost more than your toys,
My clothes are trendier too.
My school costs more than your school –
I'm much better than you.

At this point the poem comes to a terrible end
when an armed and extremely dangerous
grizzly bear, *Ursus horribilis* who is on the run
from the maximum security wing of London Zoo
and who has not eaten for three days, leaps from
behind a tree and swallows up the boy without
so much as a "How do you do?"
Sad, eh?

**Colin McNaughton**

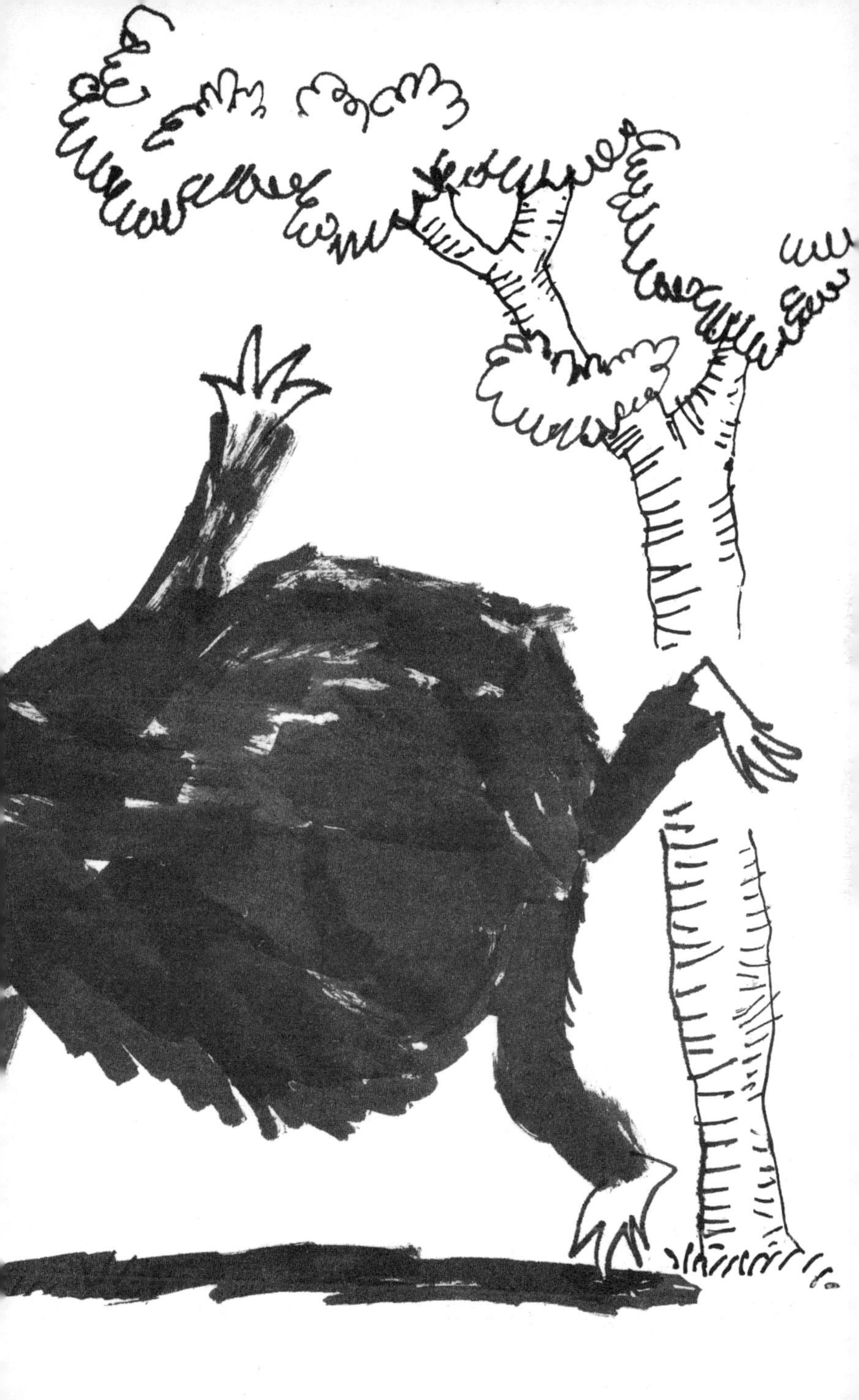

# Big Bear and Little Bear

Said Big Bear to Little Bear:
  *What are you doing,*
  *Small Brother Bruin?* –
  "Looking for honey,
  Yellow and runny!
  Star clusters humming
  Are brimming the comb
  In the hive of the air,
  Going and coming,
  And I'll never go home
  Till I've licked the sky bare."

Said Big Bear to Little Bear:
  *When will you get it?* –
  "When cupids start singing
  And chimes begin ringing
  And kisses are clinging
  And sweethearts are young.
  When I have eaten it
  Without any spoon
  I'll hang out my tongue
  Till the next honey moon."

**Eleanor Farjeon**

# Algy Met a Bear

Algy met a bear,

A bear met Algy.

Bulgy Bear

Algy

The bear was bulgy,

The bulge was Algy.

**Anon**

# The Brown Bear

In the winter,
When the cold winds blow,
When the land is covered with snow.
The brown bear sleeps.

In winter,
When the nights come soon,
When the land
Freezes beneath the moon.
The brown bear dreams.

The brown bear
Dreams of summer heat,
Of berries,
Honey and nuts to eat.
The brown bear sighs.

The brown bear
Stirs, then digs down deep,
Safe and sound
In its winter sleep.
The brown bear dreams.

**John Foster**

# Song of a Bear

There is a danger where I move my feet.

I am a whirlwind.

There is a danger where I move my feet;

I am a grey bear.

When I walk, where I step lightning flies from me.

Where I walk, one to be feared.

Where I walk, long life.

One to be feared I am.

There is a danger where I walk.

**Navajo, North American Indian**

71

# The Bear

Chained to his pole, the dancing bear
Waltzes across the village square.

His keeper skips along the middle
Scraping a tune on an old cracked fiddle.

With leather boots and scarlet shirt
He leads the creature through the dirt.

The greatest beast lumbers round and round
While coins are flung upon the ground.

Pity the clumsy dancing bear
Who used to breathe the forest air.

**Gerard Benson**

# Home from the Carnival

Gone all the lights and all the noise,
Gone all the cotton candy's joys
And all my money spent and gone
With all the rides I rode upon
And all my money gone and spent
Upon the tables in the tent:
The Wheel of Fortune clicked and spun –
I lost my dimes and nothing won,
Not even from the bottom shelf.
I bring home nothing but myself
And take to bed with meagre cheer
The teddy bear I won last year.

**Russell Hoban**

P.S. If you've ever wondered about the
Koala, here's the last word on the matter:

## The Koala

In its native land the Koala
Is never called a Koala *Bear*;
That would be unfair
Because it isn't a bear.
In their accuracy
The Australians have far outstripped us;
It's a nocturnal marsupial that eats eucalyptus.

**Gavin Ewart**

# Bear Facts

- Bears hum when they are happy!

- The giant panda has a huge appetite for bamboo and a typical adult spends half the day eating.

- The scientific term for collecting teddy bears is arctophily.

- The world's smallest teddy bear is 9mm tall.

- The world's largest teddy bear is 19m tall and is called Evan.

- Standing on its hind legs, an average-sized male brown bear may reach 2m.

- 40% of adults still have their childhood teddy bear.

- A collection of teddy bears is often referred to as a "hug" of bears.

- Brown bears are often called "grizzly bears" because the tips of the hair on them is a greyish colour or "grizzled".

- Polar bears avoid slipping on ice due to the rough texture of their paw pads.

- During hibernation, black bears can go without food for up to 7 months.

- Mischievous little yellow bear, Sooty, is the star of the longest-running children's show EVER!

- Morris Michtom from Brooklyn sold the world's first "Teddy's Bear" in 1902.

- The name "teddy bear" comes from the United States President, Theodore Roosevelt whose nickname was "Teddy".

- The world's first teddy bear space flight took place in 2008, with the teddy bears surviving temperatures of -35°C.

- 2002 marked the 100th birthday of the teddy bear.

- Polar bears' fur is not white – each hair is actually a transparent hollow tube.

- Polar bears are considered to be marine mammals.

- The panda was not officially classed as a bear until 1995.

# Acknowledgements

**Furry Bear** (excerpt) by A.A. Milne from *Now We Are Six* by A.A. Milne. Text copyright © The Trustees of the Pooh Properties 1928. Published and by permission of Egmont UK Ltd London.
**The Bestest Bear Song** by Wes Magee is reprinted by kind permission of the author. Copyright © Wes Magee 1993.
**Sir Grizzly** by John Agard from *We Animals Would Like a Word With You*. Copyright © 1998. Reprinted by permission of Random House.
**Hair-Bear** by Christopher Reid from *Alphabicycle Order*. Copyright © 2001.
**Polar Bear** by Spike Milligan from *Startling Verse for all the Family* by Spike Milligan. By permission of Spike Milligan Productions Ltd.
**Runny Honey** by Adrian Mitchell from *Zoo of Dreams* published by Orchard Books. None of Adrian Mitchell's poems should be used for any examination purposes whatsoever.
**The Small Brown Bear** by Michael Baldwin from *A First Book of Poetry*. Copyright © Michael Baldwin 1979. Reproduced by permission of PFD on behalf of Michael Baldwin.
**The Brown Bear** by Roger Stevens from *Why Otters Don't Wear Socks*. Reprinted by kind permission of the poet and Macmillan Children's Books, London, UK.
**A Cold Snack** by Richard Edwards from *Whispers from a Wardrobe*. Copyright © 1987. Reprinted by permission of Lutterworth Press.
**Paws** by Stanley Cook from *The Squirrel in Town*. Copyright © 1988.
**Introduction** and **Little Barbara** by Colin West. Copyright © Colin West 2010.
**Roberta Hyde** by Mark Burgess from *Feeling Beastly*. Text copyright © Mark Burgess 1989. Published and by permission of Egmont UK Ltd London.
**5 Ways to Stop Grizzly Bears from Spoiling Your Picnic** by Roger McGough from *Bad Bad Cats*. Copyright © Roger McGough 1997. Reprinted by permission of PFD on behalf of Roger McGough.
**Rare Bear** by Hiawyn Oram. Copyright © Hiawyn Oram 1990.
**On a Trip Through Yellowstone** by X.J. Kennedy. Copyright © X.J. Kennedy 1990. First appeared in *Fresh Brats*, published by Margaret K. McElderry Books. Reprinted by permission of Curtis Brown Ltd.
**A Bear is Not Disposed** by Jack Prelutsky. Text copyright © Jack Prelutsky 2008. Reprinted by permission of HarperCollins Publishers.
**I'm Much Better Than You** by Colin McNaughton from *There's an Awful Lot of Weirdos in Our Neighbourhood*. Copyright © 1982.
**Big Bear and Little Bear** by Eleanor Farjeon from *The Starry Floor*. Reprinted by kind permission of Michael Joseph.
**The Brown Bear** by John Foster from *Snow Poems* edited by John Foster (Oxford University Press, 1990). Copyright © John Foster 1990. Reprinted by kind permission of the author.
**The Bear** by Gerard Benson from *The Magnificent Callisto*. Copyright © Gerard Benson 1992.
**Home from the Carnival** by Russell Hoban from *The Pedalling Man*. Reprinted by kind permission of William Heinemann.
**The Koala** by Gavin Ewart. Reprinted by kind permission of Margo Ewart.
**Bear Facts** collated by Caroline White.

Every reasonable effort has been made to trace the ownership of and/or secure permission for the use of copyrighted material. If notified of any omission, the publisher will gladly make the necessary correction in future printings.